For Owen, I'm thankful for you! —A.W.P.

Especially for Carolina —D.W.

Farrar Straus Giroux Books for Young Readers
An imprint of Macmillan Publishing Group, LLC
120 Broadway, New York, NY 10271

Text copyright © 2020 by Ann Whitford Paul
Pictures copyright © 2020 by David Walker
All rights reserved
Color separations by Bright Arts (H.K.) Ltd.
Printed in China by Toppan Leefung Printing Ltd., Dongguan City, Guangdong Province
Designed by Aram Kim
First edition, 2020

1 3 5 7 9 10 8 6 4 2

mackids.com

Library of Congress Cataloging-in-Publication Data is available.
ISBN: 978-0-374-31341-8

Our books may be purchased in bulk for promotional, educational, or business use.
Please contact your local bookseller or the Macmillan Corporate and Premium Sales Department
at (800) 221-7945 ext. 5442 or by email at MacmillanSpecialMarkets@macmillan.com.

If Animals Gave Thanks

Ann Whitford Paul
Pictures by David Walker

Farrar Straus Giroux
New York

If animals gave thanks,
when temperatures fell,
Rabbit would rumble a thank-you purrrrrrrrrr
for the spring in his hop and the thick of his fur.

Squirrel would **squeeeak** for her tail she can puff up over her head—an umbrella of fluff.

And Bear . . .
sensing summer was over,
would gratefully gather clumps of sweet clover.

If animals gave thanks,
when wild winds **whooshed**,
Crow would
caw-CAW for the
great bowl of sky—

his playground to swoop, **loop-de-loop**, and fly.

Raccoon would **chir-chirrrrr**
thanks for her cub
and **nuz-nuzzle** him
and **rub rubbi-rub**.

And Bear . . .
would be grateful for Honeybee
leading him to the hive in the tree.

If animals gave thanks,
when leaves fluttered down,
Frog would croak loudly—cro-oak-cro-oak—
for her bug-catching tongue and her lily-pad boat.

Beaver would yip for his tail like an oar,
thankful it steers him pad-paddling to shore.

And Bear . . .

would **shuf-shuffle**, grateful to pick
a basket of berries—**pickity-pick**.

If animals gave thanks,
when branches turned bare,
Turtle would **click** for his hard-shell dome—
thankful he never had to leave home.

Skunk would **hiss-hiss** for her stinky spray.

Coyote would **HOWLLLLL** thanks for the bright, sunny day.

And Bear . . .
would paw in the lake, **swish-swish**,
grateful to catch a gigantic fish.

Then he'd grill that fish and busily bake
berry pies and a honey cake.

He'd brew clover tea
and invite his friends, too.
They'd chitter and chatter,
chomp-chomp,
chewy-chew.

Then basking in the brisk fall weather,
they'd give thanks for their bounty
and for being together.